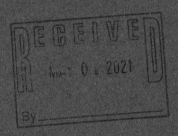

written by Germano Zullo
illustrated by Albertine

my
little
one

translated by Katie Kitamura

*elsewhere
editions*

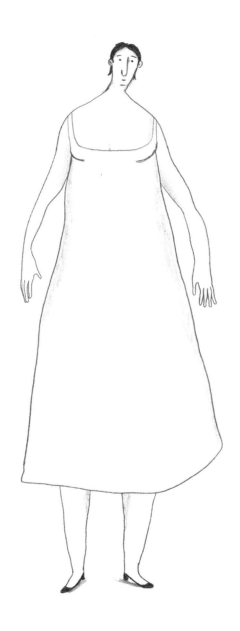

Here you are …

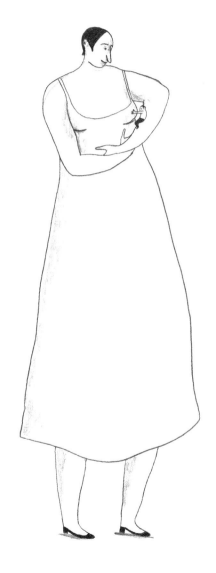

Finally!

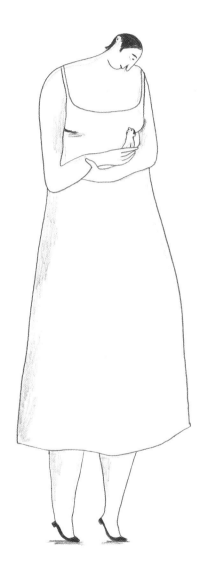

I've been waiting for you.

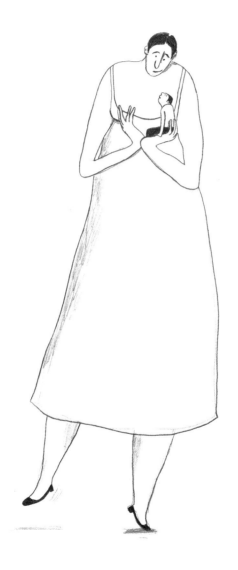

My baby, my child, my little one!

You're here now.

With me.

I love you.

And you know what?

I have so many things to tell you.

So, so many things.

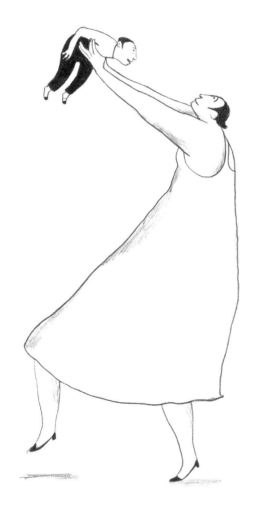

I need to tell you everything.

Everything.

I must tell you everything.

From start to finish.

It's very important.

You know?

My baby, my child, my little one!

It's a long story.

A little complicated in places.

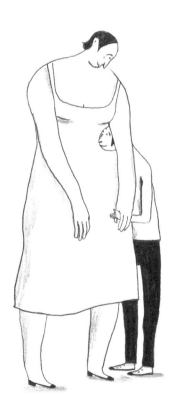

But essentially very simple.

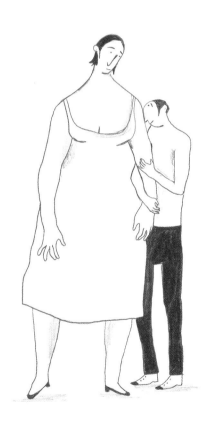

It's a story.

An epic story.

Our story.

And it's beautiful.

Even if there's not really a beginning.

Or an end.

Much less a middle.

And even if I don't really know where to start.

You see?

This story.

It's a little peculiar.

But that's how it is.

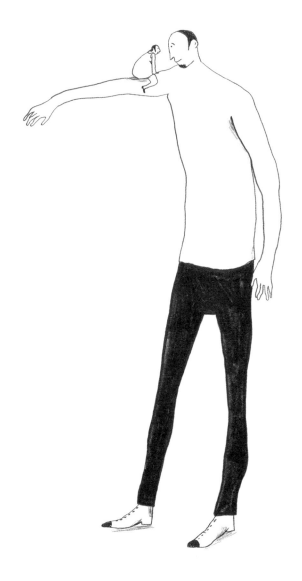

It's our story.

And when I've told it to you.

It will be a part of you.

Forever.

My baby, my child, my little one!

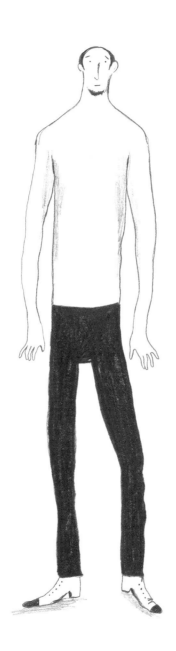

Elsewhere Editions
232 3rd Street #A111
Brooklyn, NY 11215
www.elsewhereeditions.org

Distributed by Penguin Random House
www.penguinrandomhouse.com

Funding for the translation of this book was provided by
a grant from the Carl Lesnor Family Foundation.

This work was made possible by the New York State Council on the Arts
with the support of Governor Andrew M. Cuomo
and the New York State Legislature.

Archipelago Books also gratefully acknowledges the generous support of
Lannan Foundation, Pro Helvetia, the National Endowment for the Arts,
and the New York City Department of Cultural Affairs.

PRINTED IN CHINA BY TOPPAN LEEFUNG